COMING HOME

A STORY OF JOSH GIBSON, BASEBALL'S GREATEST HOME RUN HITTER

BY NANETTE MELLAGE

ILLUSTRATED BY CORNELIUS VAN WRIGHT AND YING-HWA HU

SCHOLASTIC INC.

New York   Toronto   London   Auckland   Sydney
Mexico City   New Delhi   Hong Kong   Buenos Aires

For my brother "Dondi," who kept on pitching till I finally hit the ball —NM

For Pebbles, believing in your gift —CVW & YH

ISBN 0-439-71693-4

12 11 10 9 8   10/0

Printed in the U.S.A.   40

First Scholastic printing, February 2005

The best hitter I ever saw? Bet here's one you won't know. He played many years ago for the Homestead Grays, a Negro League team in Homestead, Pennsylvania. Josh Gibson was his name.

In those days segregation was the law of the land. Blacks and whites lived in separate neighborhoods, went to separate schools, even rode in separate sections of the same bus. It was no different with baseball, so white players had the major leagues and black players had the Negro Leagues.

The Negro Leagues had a lot of great players. Josh Gibson, Buck Leonard, Satchel Paige, and Smokey Joe Williams were as well known to Negro League fans as Babe Ruth, Lou Gehrig, and Ty Cobb were to major-league fans.

Pop took me to every home game the Grays played. I was ten when Josh joined the team. He was just eighteen years old, but to me he looked like a giant. And was that man fast! By the time the outfielders chased down what he'd hit, Josh would already be on third base.

He was also powerful—so big and so strong that everybody took to calling him Thunder. Each time Josh was up to bat we yelled, "Thunder's comin'!" It didn't take the fielders long to figure out what that meant—Josh hit hard.

The year they signed Josh was one of the best ever for the Grays. They whipped all comers and won eleven games out of twelve on a barnstorming tour against the Kansas City Monarchs. We called them the "Kings of the East" because it looked to us like there was no one left to beat.

Then along came John Henry Lloyd. He was the shortstop and manager for the New York Lincoln Giants. The Giants had also completed a winning season, so Lloyd challenged the Grays to a ten-game series to see which team would be the Negro League champions.

Nearly everybody in town turned out for the series opener. The Grays took the first game with a score of 9–1. In the second game Josh did us proud with a home run over the center-field fence! The next four games were played out of town, so Pop had to buy the *Pittsburgh Courier* and turn straight to the sports page to find out what we'd missed.

The Grays were ahead of Lincoln four games to two. Game seven was going to be played at the famous Yankee Stadium. Pop couldn't stand to miss out on that game. He decided it was a good time for us to pay a visit to my Uncle Ray in New York.

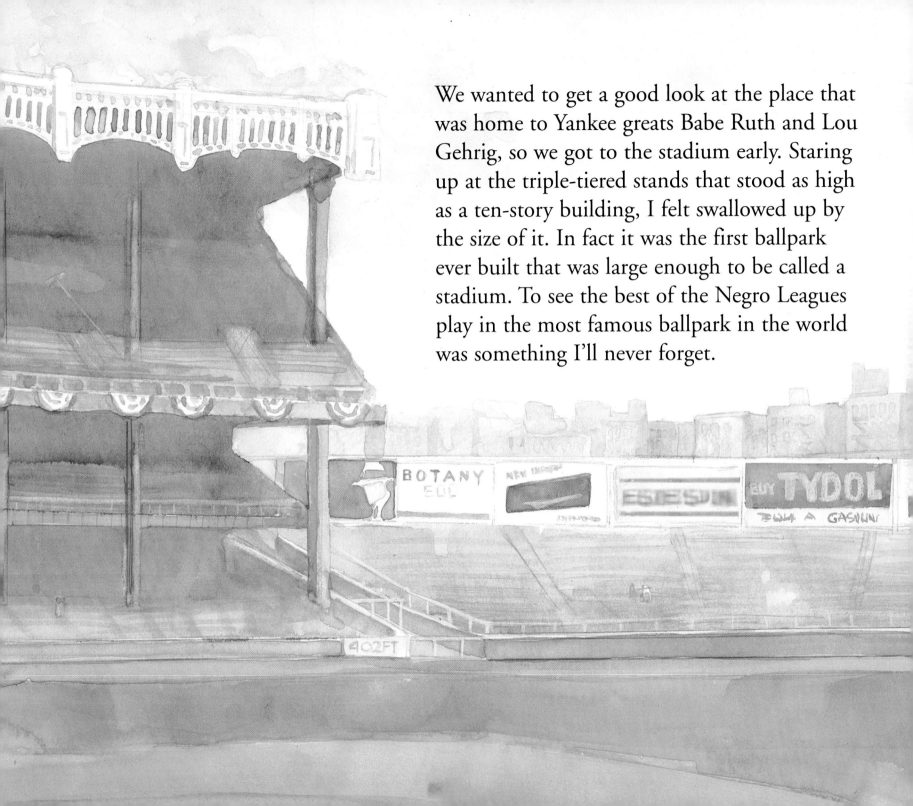

We wanted to get a good look at the place that was home to Yankee greats Babe Ruth and Lou Gehrig, so we got to the stadium early. Staring up at the triple-tiered stands that stood as high as a ten-story building, I felt swallowed up by the size of it. In fact it was the first ballpark ever built that was large enough to be called a stadium. To see the best of the Negro Leagues play in the most famous ballpark in the world was something I'll never forget.

Some of the players were warming up on the field. I spotted Josh right away and called out, "Hey, Josh, will you hit a home run for us today?" He came up to us and said, "I'm sure gonna try!" He gave me his autograph and shook Pop's hand. The smile on Pop's face was just about the biggest anyone ever had, I reckon. We could have gone home then and there — a day just couldn't get any better than that.

But it sure could get worse. From the outset the Lincoln team had the Grays on the run. Their starting pitcher was Luther Farrell. He was one of the finest pitchers in the league and was at the top of his game that day. Time and again our Homestead boys struck out.

We were all feeling a little down when Josh came to the plate for the fourth time. He hadn't got a single hit off Farrell the whole game. Farrell let go a third pitch, and Josh swung his mighty arms. Strike three. When Josh went back to the dugout and laid his bat down, my heart sank right along with it. The Grays were trailing, and things didn't look to be getting any better. Pop was so nervous he took off his hat and nearly bent it in two.

At the top of the ninth John Henry Lloyd sent Broadway Rector to the pitcher's mound. Broadway had a slow ball that could fake out some of the best sluggers in the league. So when he stepped onto the field, the Lincoln crowd went wild.

Josh was up to bat again. As he walked to the batter's box I could hear people saying, "That kid can't hit!" and "Go ahead, Broadway, hand the boy back to his mama."

Pop must have heard it, too, because he got mad—real mad. He stood up right in the middle of everybody and yelled, "Look out, now! Thunder's comin'!" Then I heard somebody else shout, "Thunder's comin'!" I got up, too, and soon all the Grays fans stood up, shouting, "Thunder's comin'!" I don't know if Josh heard us, but down in the batter's box he looked like he was standing even taller than usual.

Broadway waited for what seemed like the longest time. When he finally let go of the ball, it moved so slow a couple of folks looked at their watches, wondering if it would get past home plate before dark. Josh didn't budge. The ball kept crawling toward him, getting slower all the time. I was sure he was faked out when . . . POW! The bat was just a blur.

Everyone jumped up, trying to catch sight of the ball as it zoomed past left-center field and kept on going.

Up and up it went, until it hit the back wall of the bullpen and disappeared . . . right out of Yankee Stadium!

Well, even the Lincoln fans had to put their hands together for Josh. Everybody in the stands was clapping and cheering, "Come on home, boy! Come on home!"

Josh was a fast runner, but just this once he took his time, trotted to every base and grasped every outstretched hand.

Pop's hat was so twisted up he couldn't wear it anymore, so he just threw it in the air and shouted, "Come on home!"

No player in any league, before or since, has hit the ball as far as Josh did that day. As for me, I have yet to see a finer sight than that afternoon in September 1930, when Thunder came on home.

Author's Note

The Homestead Grays were considered the "Kings of the East" after winning eleven out of twelve games played on tour in 1930. The only team then mighty enough to challenge them was the New York Lincoln Giants. Led by John Henry "Pop" Lloyd, the Giants battled the Grays in a ten-game series for the unofficial Negro League Championship of 1930.

The series opener was a doubleheader in Pittsburgh. The Grays won the first game 9–1. The second game was a ten-inning slugfest, where Gibson hit a 457-foot home run over the center-field fence and helped the Grays to a 17–16 victory. The next afternoon in New York, the two teams split a doubleheader.

Game five brought the teams to Philadelphia's Bigler Field, where Gibson smashed the longest home run ever seen in the park's history, helping the Grays to a 13–7 win. Game six went to the Lincolns, sending the series back to New York. It was in game seven that Gibson slammed Connie "Broadway" Rector's slow ball into the left-field bullpen at Yankee Stadium. The Grays were trailing far behind, however, and even Josh's spectacular homer couldn't give them the win. The Grays won two of the remaining three games, thereby claiming the rights to the Negro League Championship.

About Josh Gibson

Josh Gibson was born on December 21, 1911, in Buena Vista, Georgia. He grew up in Pittsburgh, where his father worked in a steel mill. Josh and his younger siblings were able to attend school, which was a privilege denied many African American children at that time.

His peers described Josh Gibson as friendly, polite, and cheerful, even though his early success was marred by personal tragedy. At seventeen Josh married Helen, his childhood sweetheart. The following year Helen died while giving birth to their twin son and daughter. Leaving the babies with his mother-in-law, Josh went on the road with the Grays to earn what he could to support his new family.

Life on the road in the Negro Leagues was not easy, especially during the years Gibson played. The Great Depression took its toll on everyone. Because of segregation there were few hotels or restaurants that would accommodate black people, so teams on the road often slept in the bus. Josh was very sensitive to the injustice he and his teammates faced every day. When black teams played white teams in exhibition games, things occasionally got rough.

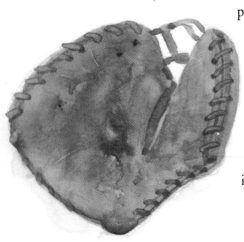

Despite all the hardships, Josh never lost his love for baseball. He always held out hope that the major leagues would become integrated and he would have the opportunity to play. However, Josh's health was rapidly deteriorating. In 1947, at the age of thirty-five, Josh Gibson died of a stroke. Three months after his death, Jackie Robinson was hired to play for the Brooklyn Dodgers, and the color line in major-league baseball was finally broken.